TY
THE HUNTER

THE
WORLD
KEEPERS

-BOOK 1-

THE WORLD KEEPERS

BOOK 1

TY THE HUNTER

For my boys.
Without you guys,
my life would be a whole lot more boring.
But I'd never have to shave the dog.

The World Keepers Series

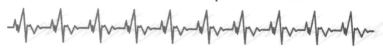

Visit TyTheHunter.com for updates and to download your FREE book, "The World Keepers - Beginnings".

Also, don't forget to leave a review once you've finished the book. The more reviews you leave, the more books I write.

Get in touch with me at theworldkeepersbooks@gmail.com

Chapter 1

Set In Jed's Room
Middle Of The Day

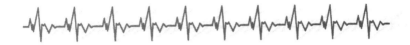

My name is Jed.

Okay, well, no, my name isn't Jed exactly, but that's what everyone calls me.

It's so much easier that way. I mean, if you had a name like Augustus Jedediah Bartholomew Barrington, you'd go for the nickname too, right?

It seems my parents had a tough time when they were deciding who to name me after.

First, there was my great grandfather, Augustus, on my dad's side.

Then, there was Uncle Jedediah, three times removed on my mother's side. He may or may not have been related to a president.

To this day, I have no idea where Bartholomew comes from. I think Mom and Dad just liked *The Simpsons* and thought they'd have a laugh at my expense.

They tried calling me "Gus" for a while, but too many people went, "Oh, like the mouse in Cinderella?"

For the record, no, not like the fat, doofy looking mouse in Cinderella.

I'm not sewing any dresses, and I don't sing.

Thank goodness they never tried calling me "Bart"! You show me one person who doesn't hear the name "Bart" and automatically think of that cartoon spiky-haired brat, and I'll show you someone who is lying their pants off.

So, Jed it was. By process of elimination, this is who I am.

Unless I'm in trouble, then I get all four names. You know how that goes.

Sometimes I find it funny, such a long name for plain old me. I mean I'm pretty fantastic as far as kids go, don't get me wrong. I'm cool, I'm funny, and I can jump higher than any of my friends. I also tell a mean knock-knock joke, but other than that stuff there's nothing super special going on here.

I like to think I'm saving up all the epic for when I get older.

Anyway, where was I?

Oh yes, I'm 10 years old, and I have an older brother named Thomas. I hate school (who doesn't?), and I love Netflix, "Minecraft", "Roblox", and pretty much any tank or warship game you throw my way.

I'm just over five feet tall, I'm skinny, and I have light brown hair in a constant buzz cut (thanks, Mom). I have blue eyes, get a tan by just THINKING about sunshine, and shorts are my preferred article of clothing. If you see me in long pants, it's because my mom made me wear them and we're probably going someplace fancy.

See? I'm just your average Joe ... err Jed.

This story isn't about me, though, not really. At least it wasn't supposed to be about me.

More on that later.

It's about my older brother, Thomas, and all the weird stuff that's been going on with him lately. Let me tell you about him, and then I'll get into the rest of the story, get you all caught up.

Let's see. Where should I start?

Thomas is 12 but practically 13. We look a lot alike, only he's taller than me by like six inches. Everyone always remarks that he looks so much older than 12, even older than 13. It's because he's a beanpole. He's pretty cool as far as older brothers go, and he kicks butt at video games! He plays "Roblox", "Minecraft", "Call of Duty", "Battlefield", any of the Lego games, and he rocks them all!

One day, I'm going to beat him. I get frustrated with how much better he is than me, but Mom assures me he was WAY worse when he was my age. I really am trying not to dwell on it so much, but I can't wait to pound him into the digital dirt!

Despite him always winning, I do love playing video games with him. The problem is that he doesn't love playing with me. He gets frustrated when I take too long or when I mess up some strategy he's using for one thing or another.

I have very little patience for him complaining to me, so it ends with us fighting. Controllers get thrown, and then Mom gets involved, my iPad gets taken away... You get the idea.

It turns out we don't play a whole lot of video games together.

Up until a few weeks ago, that didn't bother me too much. We did other stuff together, so it was all right. We've got a yard that's huge. It's almost 3 acres, and it's all fenced in. We'd race each other outside and have epic Nerf gun battles or build stick forts or attach sheets to skateboards and ride them down the driveway. We'd even draw intricate race tracks with sidewalk chalk and then race our RC cars around on them.

Basically, despite us not getting along in the video game world, we still did a lot of other things together.

Then it stopped, practically overnight.

Thomas changed.

He started staying in his room more and playing on his computer more. He also began keeping his door locked and getting mad at me when I'd try to come in and hang out. He stopped talking to me. He stopped playing outside with me, and he started looking tired and stressed out all the time.

I know what you're thinking; he's 12, it's probably hormones, right? Like he's about to hit the big P (that's puberty if you didn't know), so he's going to act like a jerk from now until the time he moves out.

At least that's what my mom says is going to happen.

That's not it, though. I know my brother, and I know when something is wrong as opposed to when he's just being a moody brat.

Right now, something is very, very wrong.

He and I have rooms in the same hallway, right across from one another. We're the only two in that part of the house, and I hear him up at night, moving around, doing … things. Sometimes I'd even swear I hear him talking to people, or a person, I don't know. I can only hear his side of it so it could be he's just talking to himself, but I doubt it.

At first, I thought he was making a bunch of noise at night because he was going pee all the time. Like, "Hey dude, lay off the water before bedtime!" Lifehack there. You're welcome.

But, see, the bathroom is right next to my room, so if Thomas were going in there, I'd know about it. I'd hear the toilet flushing, the water running, the door opening and closing, something.

There's nothing, though, other than the odd sounds and strange light coming from his room long after we're supposed to be asleep.

It doesn't take much to connect the dots. He starts acting weird and weird things start happening in his room at night, the two have got to be related.

I've asked him about it, of course, but he just looks at me like I'm being annoying. He never answers my questions, so he's left me no choice.

I'm not trying to be a snoopy little brother; I'm not that guy. I'm worried about him though. If something is going on and I could have helped him, what kind of brother would I be if I ignored it?

I've got to stop writing for now, Mom's calling, dinner's ready. After that, it's a few more hours until bedtime, and then it's on.

Tonight's the night; one way or another, I'm going to figure out what's going on with Thomas.

Chapter 2

Middle Of The Night
The House Is Asleep

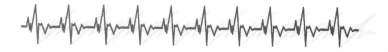

beep!!! beep!!!! beep!!!!!!!!!! beep!!!!!! SMACK!

I fling my arm over my face then put it back under the blanket because the air is cold. Rolling over in my bed I squint at my alarm clock, making sure I smacked it in the right place to shut it off instead of snooze. Is it early or late? I have no idea what you'd consider 3 a.m., but I don't like it.

There's a moment of indecision where I snuggle back down into my cozy blankets, pulling them back up to my chin. It would be so easy just to roll over and go back to sleep. I'm so warm; it's so much colder in the hallway. I'm going to get goose bumps. Heck,

I'm getting goose bumps just thinking about it.

"No, Jed." I start an internal pep talk. "This is important; you need to figure out what's up with Thomas." If I figure out what's going on, he will have to talk to me, and I can help him.

I'll even keep it from my parents if that's what he's worried about.

I mean as long as he's not breaking the law, I can deal.

I could even deal if he were breaking the law, maybe. Okay, total honesty here; it would depend on which law.

Kidding!

Well, sort of.

Committed, I kick my legs over the side of my bed and grab a pair of wool socks I've left on the carpet, sliding them on to my still warm feet. I'm a hot sleeper, underwear in bed type of guy, so I also have to put on a pair of sweatpants and a T-shirt.

The last thing I want to do is wake up Thomas because my teeth are chattering.

Before heading out of my room, I run down a mental checklist of things I might need.

1. Socks (for silence)
2. iPad (for flashlight feature, and picture taking)
3. Blanket
4. Backpack (for any proof I find)

My priority is SILENCE!

Thomas might be asleep in there, but I don't know what kind of sleeper he is, light or heavy. And while his room isn't small, it's also not huge. I've got to sneak around, especially since I'll be sneaking around while he snores in his bed just a few feet from me.

Not joking here, he really does snore. He also talks in his sleep.

I remember going on vacation with my grandmother once, she was on the pull out couch by herself. Thomas and I each had our own twin bed, but we were all in the same room.

The next morning, she told us that Thomas had woken her up from a sound sleep by going, "Ring a ding, ding, ding, ding!" in the middle of the night. She said it scared the life out of her. At first, she thought he was messing around, but when she checked on him, he was out like a light.

It still makes me laugh when I think about it.

RING A DING, DING, DING, DING! I yell that at him when I see him sometimes.

So I'm pretty sure he's a heavy sleeper, but … better to err on the side of caution.

At the last minute, I decide I can probably leave the backpack behind.

If I find something I really want to use to confront him with later, I can just walk back to my room with it. I figure I've got at least a few pictures in me before the flash wakes him up, maybe two or three. That really should be good enough.

I know you're probably wondering why I'm bringing a blanket with me, but it's all part of the plan. See, Thomas's room is always a total mess; it's downright hazardous to walk across his floor. I figure if he wakes up while I'm checking things out, I can throw the blanket over myself and pretend to be just another pile of laundry lying around.

#genius

I know it works; I've used it before during "hide and seek"! He's such a slob; he'll never even know I'm there.

I am hoping it doesn't come to that though.

My checklist is checked, my clothes are warm, and my brain is more awake than it was five minutes ago, so it's time to go.

"Quietly, Jed." I steady myself and think ninja thoughts.

I know what's coming; there are a whole lot of potential squeaks and creaks between my room and Thomas's room.

The first obstacle is my door, it makes the most awful "eeeeee!" sound every time I open it. I keep reminding myself to tell my dad so he can oil it, but my mind gets so full of other things during the day.

I never seem to think about it until I get up at night to pee.

Pushing myself out of bed, I place my feet on the carpet and step lightly to the edge. It's a plush rug in the shape of a rectangle, covering most of the floor but not all. I reach the end and stop stepping, it's quieter to start sliding my socked feet across the wood.

The brushed nickel door knob is chilly beneath my hand. When I wrap my fingers around it, a shiver runs up my spine. We're in a cold front, it hasn't gotten above 20 degrees in the last week, which is insane for us Texas folk. Despite the thermostat being set at 70 all the time, this metal is icy cold.

It only adds to how nervous I am about the whole thing.

No matter how nervous I am, though, my intentions are good. Thomas is in trouble, I can feel it in my bones. Something big is going on. Something is changing him from a happy, fun person into a miserable, moody ball of suck.

I open my door, and *creeeeaaaaakkkk*!

Agh! No matter how carefully I open it, that always happens. Of course, tonight would be no exception.

Abandoning my earlier bravery, I leave the door open a crack, rush/slide back into bed, and cover myself with the blankets. You know, just in case Thomas is still up (doing whatever he's been doing) and decides to investigate the noise.

A full minute passes as I lie there, counting down from 60 ... 59 Mississippi, 58 Mississippi, 57 Mississippi ... all the way to one Mississippi. I keep waiting for the telltale sound of feet on the floor or the sound of his door being flung open.

No one comes through, everything is silent; the house continues its slumber.

With my door now open a crack, I can see that familiar light coming from Thomas's room. It pulses in a slow rhythm, red ... white ... dark, then again, red ... white ... dark. It's bright enough that it's casting shadows on my wall and I wonder how my parents have never noticed it.

After being back in bed for a few minutes it's obvious that my courage is starting to fail me a little bit, so I sit up and put my feet on the carpet once again.

It's time to get this over with.

I move quickly this time, like the bear in the story my mom used to read to me. "Out the door, in the box, up the hill," etc. Only for me, it's "Out of bed, across the floor, to the door." I touch the edge with the tips of my fingers and ease it further open, moving silently into the night time hallway.

It's "do or die" time, no more turning back.

Taking the last few steps to Thomas's door, I suck in a breath and grip my iPad tighter in my hand. My "hide me" blanket gets tossed over my shoulder; then I grab the knob and twist.

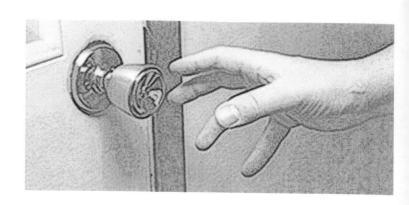

Chapter 3

Jed Stands In The Hallway Ready To Sneak Into Thomas's Room

My heart is beating right out of my chest as I steal into Thomas's dark, stinky lair. Thankfully, his door has never squeaked, it must be because he slams it so hard every time he shuts it. There's no resistance; it just swings silently into the intermittent darkness.

How does he sleep with this going on? It would drive me nuts!

The pulsing red light is just bright enough to disorient me, changing the way things look. It keeps my night vision from coming entirely into focus, making my search so much harder.

The first thing I do is cast a glance at his bed, just to make sure he's sleeping. With the light going bright to dark and his bedding being a black blanket with black sheets, I can't see a thing. If he weren't asleep, he'd have busted me by now, so I'm going to assume he is.

I glance around the room, keeping my mental map at the ready. It's a perfect square, except for a 3' x 5' cubby cut out to the left of the door. It was supposed to hold his desk, but, since Thomas is a slob, the desk isn't where it should be.

Let's see; there's a low bed right in front of me and a set of 3' x 3' high cube shelves on the right.

His computer is on a blue desk set by the back wall near the window, and there is a large, red plastic toy box on the right wall. It's got a giant, red tub with two blue drawers underneath and a large, blue plastic top that you can close or remove.

Sometimes, when Thomas is doing his schoolwork, I see him lie in bed and grab the top of the toy box to use as a desk. I'm not sure why we still have them, really. We don't need that kind of storage anymore. I guess it's a throwback to when we were much smaller and had lots of huge toys that Mom had to find a place for.

Creeping slowly in, I keep glancing down to make sure I'm not about to step on anything. I'm not so worried about kicking something into a wall; I'm being too careful for that. It's just that we both have a lot of small electronics, and I could easily step on one, making it beep or flash.

He actually might not even notice the flashing, since that's already happening, but the noise...

I get all the way to the middle of the room without making any noise. I'm feeling pretty confident about looking around, so I let my blanket drop to the floor but hang on to my iPad. Maybe I can wake up his computer and see what's on his screen. There must be something—incriminating text messages, questionable browser history? I could take a picture of it or even take a screenshot and text it to myself.

Wait, no, terrible idea. If I text it to myself, he'll know I was in here.

Still, the computer sounds like the place to start, so that's where I'm going.

Thomas's bed is very low to the ground, one of those wooden platform setups that have no storage underneath. If you lie on it, you can reach the ground with no effort at all. If you try to put your hand under the bed, you'll just ram your fingers into particle board.

I'm sure it's part of mom's grand plan to make him less messy, but, and I hate to burst her bubble here, it's not working. True, he might not be able to cram all his junk underneath, but that just means it's strewn all around his room instead.

She needs to face facts. Her house is going to be a mess until he moves out.

The important thing is that the bed is the perfect height for me to crack my shins on if I'm not careful.

I tiptoe further into the room, keeping an eye on the bed as I ease toward his shelves and desk. That seems to be where the light is coming from.

I figure I should check it out first, even before the computer. That way I can turn the light off. I'll do anything to minimize my chances of him seeing me if he wakes up. Once I've got some actual darkness in here, I can ruin it all over again by opening his computer.

#greatplan #iknowright

Footsteps sound in the hallway, and I freeze.

This is it, my parents are up, or Thomas was hiding and I'm about to get busted.

The footsteps I hear are getting closer, close enough for me to notice the distinct *clack, clack, clack* of dog toenails on wood. Ty (my German Shepherd) walks into Thomas's room like he owns the place. He looks up at me, wags his tail, and starts sniffing the floor near my feet. *chomp,

chomp, chomp* I'm pretty sure he just ate something. Shoot!

I say a little prayer that it wasn't one of Thomas's "Awesome Little Green Men". After a moment or two, he decides he's seen enough and pads back out. I hear him heft himself up onto the leather couch in the living room, settling back into sleep.

My heartbeat returns to normal, and I wipe the sweat off my forehead.

In a smooth motion, I continue to shuffle backward. My back is to the shelves, and my eyes are forward, letting me keep the bed in sight. I keep looking for any movement that might indicate Thomas is waking up.

I'm surprised he didn't wake up when Ty came in.

That should have been my first clue.

There's no movement, though, and I'm about to breathe a sigh of relief when I realize that there really is NO movement at all. No slight shifting of a blanket to show a breathing body underneath. There's not even a significant lump to indicate that anyone is lying down.

Despite Thomas's black bedding, I should still be able to see his face or some part of his head, even if it is shoved downward in that uncomfortable looking position he seems to prefer.

I'm still backing up, hand outstretched, ready to tap the Redstone block when my brain registers what I'm seeing, or, rather, what I'm not seeing.

Thomas is not in that bed. I look around quickly, hoping beyond hope that I just missed something. Maybe he's hiding behind his door or waiting silently in his closet, ready to go, "GOT YA!"

But no, nothing, there's no one in this room aside from me.

Enough snooping, my brain screams at me! *I need to go wake my parents! My brother is gone!*

I step forward, ready to run out of the room, and forget to look down. My foot hits a piece of sidewalk chalk Thomas left lying on the floor. The motion shoots my leg forward, and I lose my balance; my arms pinwheel backward to try to keep myself upright.

It doesn't work. I fall backward, my head smacks the Redstone block, and my world goes black.

Chapter 4

Wakey Wakey!
Why Does My Back Hurt?

I come back to consciousness in a bright room. My eyes are shut, but I can see the red of my eyelids and the blobs of shapes around me. They are moving splotches that cast dark shadows as they cross my line of sight.

There is noise, a lot of noise actually. I can hear bells ringing. They sound like the ones you hear on TV shows. You know the sitcoms that feature a high school or middle school?

The shrill "BRRRRRIIIIIINNNNNGGGG" echoes through the space.

People are shouting and laughing, and there's a clanging of metal. I can even hear the rusty push and pull of things being shoved, like a massive sliding door being opened and closed.

Footsteps sound to the front of me, lots and lots of footsteps. Like a herd of elephants stomping through a cave.

Also, I'm freezing cold.

I shift a bit, curling up tighter to preserve my warmth. My hand seeks out the place where my blanket should be but instead meets air.

So, no blanket, no light dimming curtains, and my tailbone feels like it's resting on a bed of nails.

Reaching down, I push my fingers beneath my back, pressing down on whatever I'm lying on. It's not quite a bed of nails, but it's not far off. There is a thin mattress under my body. It's so flat and unsupportive that, when I press, I'm sure I can feel some rough texture beneath. It might be stone or a metal grate.

I open my eyes slowly, blinking rapidly against the glare of fluorescent lights. Once

I've gotten used to the brightness, I turn my head toward all the noise. I can't really see much besides what looks to be a metal … toilet. Huh, gross.

It's like 10 inches from my face, super gross.

Sitting up, I swing my legs off the mattress in one smooth motion then prop my hands straight behind me, resting my palms flat on the bed.

Once I've got my bearings, I can see that I'm on the bottom of a set of bunk beds, inside of what can only be a jail cell.

The walls are made of cinder block and painted a standard drab grey. At least I think they're painted. They might not be. They might just be cinder blocks without paint. I don't have a lot of experience with jail cells, so I'm no expert.

My suspicions about it being a jail are confirmed beyond a shadow of a doubt a moment later.

Outside the cell, a blue-uniformed guard walks by, roughly banging his nightstick on the bars in front of me. He holds the plastic grip in his palm, letting the bat end of the stick hit each and every bar on his way down the hall, creating an incredible amount of noise.

"All prisoners to the yard!" He stops in front of my cell and yells at me, making sure I take notice, as though I could have missed him.

I sit there in a stupor for a few seconds, trying to get my bearings, but have no idea what's going on. Asking him for some insight might not be the best idea, but I'm about to anyway because I can't think of anything else.

Before I have a chance to talk to him, he decides my hesitation means disrespect. His face changes into an ugly smirk, and he comes into the cell. Walking to the lower bunk, he reaches out and grabs me roughly by the collar of my orange jumpsuit, dragging me off the mattress.

"I said out to the yard. Now move it or I'll give you a little extra motivation." He gets right in my face when he talks, and I grimace.

His breath stinks like rotten cheese, and he could really do with a dental appointment.

With one last shove, just to get the point across, I guess, I find myself propelled through the cell opening.

Once there, I join a never-ending flow of prisoners. These are the elephants in the cave, no doubt about it.

We walk as one down metal ramps, passing cell after cell. Some are empty, others have prisoners in them. They see us and fall into line, like lemmings running across a field.

We have to walk for a while before we get to the yard. We're on the third floor, and each story attaches to the next by those ramps. This place is huge. I look up but can't tell how many levels there might be, maybe 12 or 15. The block walls seem to go on forever.

You've got to go slowly down or risk tripping and falling. I don't want to do either, and I certainly don't want to get trampled, so

I step carefully, keeping pace with the rest of the mob.

Ten minutes later, forever when you're scared and confused, we come to a double door set into the frame of the building. There is a keypad beside the door, and a guard in a blue uniform stands by, keeping the doors unlocked and opened. I wonder if they lock them once we're all out there. I also wonder how big the yard is. Do we do this in shifts or does everyone just head out at once?

Apparently, we do it all at once.

Walking outside, I take note of the space. It's large, acres of land enclosed by a fence. It's sort of green and sort of concrete, with areas set up for different types of recreation. There's a black top rectangle clearly meant for basketball. Another area probably used to be grass but is now mostly dirt. It contains various types of weight equipment. The prisoners over there are bulky, looking intimidating as they stand around and pump iron.

Just inside the fence, 20 feet inside or so, there's a track cut out of the grass. Prisoners are running around the track or walking along it, alone or in small groups.

The yard is crawling with orange jumpsuits and blue uniforms. It seems much more disorderly than it did back inside the building. One of the other prisoners walks by me, and I reach out a hand to stop him. "Hey man, what in the heck is this place?"

If he hears me, he takes no notice, and he doesn't bother answering my questions. Instead, he turns to me and says, "Have you tried breaking out?"

Then he walks away.

What? I think to myself. *Break out?* What kind of crazy place have I landed myself in?

I walk toward a set of weights in the yard, thinking I might talk to the guys hanging out over there. They're scary looking for sure, but maybe I can use flattery. You know, "Hello, good sir, your muscles are quite large. They glisten nicely in the sun," or something.

As I make my way there, I see something. Huh. There's a large wooden hammer on the ground by a weight bench. As I watch, one of the prisoners gets up, grabs the hammer, and slips it into the waistband of his pants. He walks away toward the track as though nothing happened.

Who leaves a freaking mallet in a prison yard? That just seems like a terrible idea! It's like they're begging people to try to escape.

Huh...

I glance around again, and things suddenly start to fall into place.

It's like a light bulb goes off in my head. I have an answer, but ... it can't really be the answer. Because if I am where I think I am, I've gone very crazy or something has gone very technically wrong.

As it stands now, there is only one thing this could be, and that is a video game. Not just any video game but one I have played many times before and watched Thomas play just as often.

No, it can't be right, there's just no way. I look around again, willing myself to figure out something different.

No other ideas make themselves known.

I have to face facts. I am totally stuck in "Roblox".

Chapter 5

Stand Still, Be Silent
Jed Could Use Some Help

I'm standing in the yard staring at my shoes, they're quite ugly. Black boots with super thick soles almost like moonboots.

Orthopedic moonboots.

Standing here seems like a waste of time, but I'm not really sure what else I should be doing. Let's be honest, it's not every day you find yourself sucked from your house and deposited into a game. It's great on screen but a whole lot scarier when it's real.

I decide that it's okay, that I'm just going to stand here and deal with my realization. Maybe, if I stay here long enough, someone will figure out that I'm concussed on Thomas's floor and take me to a hospital.

I'll wake up in a clean bed, with a fluffy mattress and crisp, white sheets. A beautiful nurse will help me sip apple juice from a cup while she smiles at me sweetly and tells me how brave I am.

My parents will fawn all over me, Mom will bake cookies, Dad will let me have an extra hour on the PS4, and Thomas will feel terrible (rightly so!). He'll let me come into his room as much as I want, he'll get back to building tent forts with me.

It'll be perfection.

I'm standing there in the middle of my daydream, grinning like an idiot, when someone digs their finger hard into my ribs and whispers, "What are you doing here?"

"YIPE!" I scream and jump in the air like a cat seeing a cucumber.

"What the heck! Why did you do that?" I whirl around and find myself face-to-face with a girl. Check that, let me elaborate, she's a PRETTY girl. Before I can check myself, I reach up and smooth my hair. Ugh, Jed! Suave! If she notices, she doesn't mention it, thank goodness. I look closely at her; she's older than me but not by much, maybe 13 or 14, my height, long, dirty-blonde hair, a cute perky nose, rosy lips, and she's dressed as a prisoner, just like me.

While she is pretty, she also looks furious, though I'm not sure why.

It's like that part in *The Lego Movie*: "Blah, blah, blah, I'm angry with you."

I smile at her, placating. "Hello to you too. Do we know each other?" Smile or no, I take a couple of steps back from the pretty girl, putting some space between us.

She walks toward me, closing the gap I just created and gets right in my face.

"No, you don't know me, and, no, I don't know you, but I know your brother, and you are NOT supposed to be here!" She takes a breath, and I'm about to ask a question, but she's not done yet. Poking her finger into my chest, she says, "You need to get out before they realize who you are!"

I rub at the spot she just poked. "Owwww..." But she takes no notice. She's still whisper/yelling at me, and people are starting to look. She takes a step back and begins walking into the building, yanking on my shirt to indicate that I should come with her.

I change my mind, she's not pretty. She's just mean.

Her timing is perfect though. She must play this game a lot because we make it to the double doors just as one of the guards yells, "Prisoners, back in your cells!"

I begin walking back in as well, mostly because she's MAKING ME, but also because I have no idea what to do otherwise. Also, I don't get the feeling she's really giving me a choice in the matter. She may be small, but she's probably not prepared to take "no" for an answer. It's cool, though, I have no clue what else to do, and at least blending in with the crowd will give me a bit of a chance to think.

The girl doesn't seem to like the fact that I'm walking behind her. She's probably afraid I'll run off if she can't see me. Either that or she wants to be within easy range to abuse me some more.

Whatever her reasoning, she slows her pace until she's walking just behind me.

As I expected, she grabs ahold of my elbow (not gently, either, mind you) and starts talking in a low voice near my ear. "Listen to me, Jed." WHOA, WHOA, she knows my name! How does she know my name? "You have got to get out of here."

I whirl on her, irritated. "Oh my gosh, news flash," I say, mimicking her snarky tone. "I would love to get out of here! I have no idea how I got in here! Actually, no, this isn't real, I am lying in a heap on Thomas's floor because he's a slob and I tripped over a piece of chalk."

She's staring at me like I'm crazy, and, honestly, I might be, but I'm on a roll.

"Now, if you can tell me how to go back home, I will GLADLY do it. If you're just going to stand here pinching, poking, and yelling at me, then I have to tell you that it's NOT HELPFUL!" There, I'm done. I walk faster, intending to get away from crazy, but she keeps hanging on to me, apparently not finished.

"If you listen to me, I will help, so just stop a second!" She pulls me to the side of the hallway, so we're standing against the cinder block walls.

"Did you see the hammer outside?" She gestures back the way we just came. "There are things like that all over this place, just like in the game. So go grab a hammer or something to hit or chisel with, then go to your cell and crack the toilet away from the floor."

She gives my arm a shake. "Are you listening? I'm literally telling you how to escape, right now!"

"Yes!" I yell (as quietly as I can). "I am listening, but I already know what to do! I've seen Thomas play this a million times! I've broken out of here myself a million times!"

"Good!" She lets go of my shirt and indicates that I should go back to my cell. "Great! Go do it then! Get out of here and get back home before you ruin everything!"

Whoa, hold up, no ma'am. "Ruin everything? What am I ruining? I'm not the one that decided to come here. I didn't just wake up and plan on being inside of a video game. Someone BROUGHT me here, do you get that?"

At this, her face changes a little. She looks uncertain, and then, if I'm not mistaken, she seems chastised, like somehow this might be her fault. "I'm not leaving without answers," I tell her, "and if I had to guess, I'd say you have those answers."

She looks down at the floor, and I know I've struck gold. She is officially someone in the know. "If Thomas is in trouble somehow," I say, "I'm going to help him. And if he's in here instead of at home, I have to help him get out."

"He's not here," she says, "and I get that you want to help him, but this isn't the way to do it. You weren't supposed to be the one that came through."

Came through? Came through where?

"Okay," I say, "listen. If I go, if I promise to break out, will you tell me what's going on?" I'm not a daredevil; I know I'm in way over my head. I also know that whatever this is it is significant, and I'd rather know about it before it sneaks up on me.

She looks at me, studying my face. "Yes, if you go now, if you promise to get home, I promise to send you a message explaining stuff."

I'm not sure if I should believe her, but I'm also not sure I have a choice.

Staying here isn't an option.

She takes my silence for indecision, so she gives me a little more to go on. "My name is Kat." She holds out her hand for me to shake.

I stare at it like it might bite me but then reach out and shake it, feeling more than a little awkward. I mean, really, we're well past the point of introductions.

"Listen," she says, "your brother is fine, but he won't be if you get captured, so you've got to go." She looks around, checking to make sure no one is listening. "As for what's going on, I can't tell you that right now, there's no time, but I will, I swear it. Please, just go. Get out of here. I'll tell Thomas to explain it all to you when you get back home."

"Or you'll do it yourself," I remind her, "right?"

"Yes or I'll do it myself," she promises again.

"Alright, I'll go, but I want answers. You tell Thomas that I want answers."

She nods and turns away from me, heading back the way we came. I push myself away from the wall, walking forward to rejoin the crowds of prisoners being led back to their cells.

Making my way up the first three ramps, I turn in the direction of my cell block. I'm trying my best to keep my eyes peeled for another hammer or anything at all so I can get ready to make my escape.

Sadly, it's not to be. I don't make it more than 10 feet toward my cell when I'm grabbed by a prison guard. He wraps both hands around my midsection and hauls me off my feet. I struggle, but he's bigger and stronger than me, and I know I'm in so much trouble.

"Well, well, who do we have here? Thomas's little brother. It must be my lucky day." The guard smirks, indicating to some other guards that they should come over and help him. "I'm taking you someplace special, kid. I hope you like the dark."

Chapter 6

In A Cinderblock Corridor
As Other Prisoners Come And Go

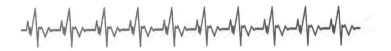

The guard—I am able to crane my head enough to see that the nametag on his shirt says, "Dirk,"—drops me back to the ground. He grabs me roughly by my collar (having people do this to me is getting old). Then he drags me down the hall of my cellblock.

I start to scramble, looking around. We're going to the very end, toward a set of offices I haven't noticed before.

They would be easy to miss, really. It's two unremarkable metal doors with a tiny window set up high in each.

As we make our way there, I dig my heels into the gridded metal floor, trying to stop his progress. My defiance makes him yank harder on my collar, bending my neck forward and putting me at an awkward angle.

It doesn't matter, though; I redouble my efforts to get away.

I kick at his legs and even attempt to sit down, anything to make this harder for him. Beyond a shadow of a doubt, if he gets me through those doors, I'll never get back home. I'll never see my parents again, I'll never see Thomas again, and I'll never see my dogs again.

The doors loom closer, 30 feet, 25 feet, 20 feet.

Suddenly, Dirk's hand on my collar goes slack, and I fall backward, onto my butt. I look up, trying to see what happened, but Dirk is no longer there. Instead, he's crumpled in a heap on the ground at my feet.

The guards he called to help him are weaving their way through prisoners, pushing and shoving them to make space. They increase their speed when they see me get up. They're shouting at me to stop, realizing I'm about to take off.

As I turn to run, I see a jogging prisoner going in the opposite direction. He's pocketing what looks like a small Taser, and he's out of sight before I can see his name. It doesn't matter who he is, I guess, but I have no doubt he just saved my life.

I seize the chance I've been given. Breaking into a run, I dart down the hallway. I take off up the closest metal ramp toward a block of cells on the next floor.

The guards behind me are in hot pursuit, still yelling and firing their weapons in my direction.

"It's a video game," I tell myself. "It's just a video game, I can't really be hurt." But I can HEAR the bullets pinging off the walls and metal of the prison. I can feel the sharp pieces of cinderblock popping off, sending shards flying through the air. The shrapnel hits me in the face, drawing real blood!

Okay, check that, I can get hurt! These bullets aren't fake! If one of those hits me, I'm dead! GAME OVER, forever.

Puffing and panting with effort, I run past cell after cell, my ugly moonboots slapping against the metal grating as I look for one that's open.

They're all closed! Someone must have called for a lockdown after I escaped!

The prisoners locked in the cells cheer or jeer as I sprint past. They smack their hands, cups or whatever they have against the bars. The noise is deafening!

I reach the end of the cellblock, run up another ramp, and continue my flight, losing hope the further up I go. Not only do I have to get away from the guards, but I also have to find something to knock over a toilet so I can crawl into the pipe.

This would be hard without someone being in hot pursuit, let alone how things stand now.

My thought process stops mid-stride as an arm shoots out of a cell and blocks my path. This time the hand grabs my sleeve instead of my collar.

It's Kat! I have never been so happy to see anyone in my whole life! I stand still as she quietly slides open the cell door, ushering me in, and then silently slides it closed again.

Footsteps pound the floor just one level down; they'll be here any minute.

"Be quiet and follow my lead," she whispers, moving toward the bed in the cell.

"Grab the pillow off the top bunk," she tells me as she bends over, moving the blankets aside on the bottom bunk as though getting ready to take a nap. I reach over her, grab the pillow and drop it down, stepping back to let her have some room.

She places it where a body would go on the bottom bunk, then pulls the sheet and blanket up. She rumples them and creates an air pocket where a person's head would be.

The bed doesn't exactly look like someone is sleeping in it, but it's better than nothing, I guess.

Done with that, she walks over to the toilet and starts to move it aside. Clearly, she's already chiseled it away from the wall.

When she pushes, it shifts reasonably smoothly across the concrete floor. Even moving it by herself, it doesn't appear to give her an issue. It must be made of some super lightweight metal.

Once the toilet is moved, I can see that there's a gap, no more than 18 inches wide. The hole leads down into some nasty looking water. I can't see the bottom of the pipe, the water is too murky. Judging by how far up the water comes toward the top, I'm just barely going to fit in there, if I do at all.

"Get in! Now!" Kat shoves me from behind, almost making me step in the pipe. I'm not ready for this! "Once you're in, just go, it's not like you can leave the pipe anyway." She smiles when she says that last part.

It's not the best time to show off her sense of humor.

#timingKat

No matter, she doesn't have to ask me twice. I step into the water, one foot then the other. I can feel it seeping into my boots, it's freezing cold and goose bumps break out all over my body. I guess the good thing is that it doesn't smell totally awful. Don't get me wrong, it still smells totally awful, so let me take that back. I should say that the good thing is it's more in a cold smelling way than in a baked smelling way. If that makes sense.

I sit my butt down in the belly of the pipe, trying to acclimate myself as the frigid water comes up over my waist. Kat's not having it. She puts her hand on my shoulder and shoves me down, forcing my back into the water. I catch my hand on the edge of the floor, holding my balance so my mouth and nose don't go under.

"I'm going! I'm going! Stop shoving me!"

"Well then, get a move on, we don't have all day, and I have to get this toilet back in place!" She tips it to the side and shows me that there's a hollow part in the base where the pipe forms. It looks like she can get in the pipe and then put her hands in that hollow to move the toilet back over the hole.

We'll be gone, but the cell will look like nothing ever happened.

I know it makes me a terrible person, but I'm relieved she's coming with me. Not that I'd wish crawling through sewage on anyone. Well, maybe I'd wish it on that Dirk guy, but not someone who was being kind to me.

Using the rubber soles of my boots, and my hands flattened against the top of the pipe, I alternately pull and push myself through, leaving enough room for Kat to get in behind me. The toilet scrapes along the floor as she moves it into place. She grunts with the effort then settles in behind me, nudging my shoulder with her foot. "Alright," she says, "let's get going."

It's hard to hear down here. I strain, trying to tell if the guards have figured out where we've gone. Water, I'm just going to call it water, I like it better that way. Water is sloshing around my face, clogging my ears, and my breathing echoes off the top of the pipe.

It feels empty and closed in at the same time.

I cannot wait to get out.

I am slow, I am wet, I am freezing, and I'm pretty sure something is slithering around in this water with me. Might be a snake, might be something shaped like a snake...

Best not to think about it.

Kat is much faster than me, and she urges me to hurry up, kicking me on the arm every few minutes. "Get a move on, pokey! The guards will know what we've done, so we're going to have to go quickly. We've got to get out of the pipes before they have a chance to get to our exit."

"I thought you said there was only one way out?" I move faster to avoid the next kick she aims my way.

"There is only one way out, but, at some point, they are going to realize we took the pipes," she says. "When they figure it out, they'll do their best to meet us at the end of the system."

We continue scooting, and I hear her move around, no doubt trying to push her face higher so she can get a good breath of air. "My goal is that we'll come out inside the prison yard," she says, huffing, "but close enough to a wall that we can reach a fence and climb over. I have a friend where the pipe ends, waiting for us to make an appearance."

I'm thinking about what she said when I begin to notice that the water level in the pipe is going down. It's no longer threatening to go in my eyes, mouth, and nose but seems to be sitting level with my shoulders. After another 50 feet, it's no longer even covering my shoes, and we're definitely moving faster.

"The pipes are angling down toward the main pool," Kat tells me. "We're almost there."

I have a nasty feeling that when she says "pool," she doesn't mean the happy, fun, summer kind.

Guess what? I'm right.

Chapter 7

Just Try Not To Think About What You're Swimming In

One second I'm hurrying as fast as I can, the next second I'm free falling. Air rushes past my face as my stomach lurches, and my arms flail wildly, automatically searching for something to grab. I hit the water feet first, landing in a pool that is most definitely NOT the happy, fun, summer kind.

SPLASH!

I hit a lot harder than I thought I would and grunt with the shock of it. Immediately, I am surrounded by stuff a person should never, ever touch, let alone swim in.

Kicking my feet, I propel myself to the surface, holding my breath and pinching my nose with one hand. I do NOT want to be submerged in this, not for any amount of time! As it is, I'm going to have to scrub the first three layers off my skin when I get home. I'll also throw away my clothes and possibly toss my computer into the trash for good measure.

"Follow me!" Kat cuts through the water in front of me.

Hardcore, I think to myself. *Her middle name is probably 'hardcore'.* The sludge and stink don't even faze her; she swims like a fish, racing toward the side.

By the time I get my head above the surface and get my bearings, she's already reached a ladder set into the base of the pool. I watch her climb quickly out.

"Come on, come on!" She leaves the pool, kneels down, and lies on her belly at the edge, dangling a hand toward the "water". Her outstretched fingers are indicating that I should reach out and grab them as soon as I'm in range.

I swim to the ladder at like half her speed (if that), and take her offered hand. I give myself points for resisting the urge to pull her right back into this mess. Then I climb out and shake myself like a dog. It really doesn't help, not at all.

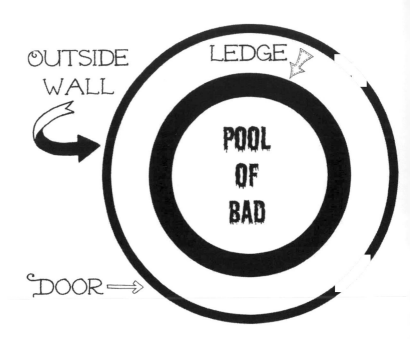

"Where to now?" I pluck my ruined clothes away from my body as much as I can. She doesn't answer, so I look up. She's already well away from me, walking quickly around the edge of the pool. There appears to another ladder resting on the outside edge. As I watch, she disappears over the side, out of view.

"Come on!" She pokes her head over the ledge and throws one hand up in the air. Apparently she's dissatisfied that I'm no longer keeping pace.

Following her lead, I run along the outer edge. It's a lip that surrounds the pool, for what reason I cannot imagine. I mean it's not as though someone is coming in here and cleaning or doing maintenance.

Wouldn't that be the worst job ever though?

About halfway around the lip, I see the ladder. It goes all the way down to the ground, ending in some sort of kitty litter looking gravel. It's pretty tall, which means I'm standing on about 20 feet of liquid gross. I kick my leg over and begin the climb down then look around for Kat because she's gone again.

#shocker

"Over here, Jed!" I hear her yell, but I can't tell which side she's yelling from. I start walking, figuring I'll run into her, since I'm going in a circle and all.

When I get to her, she's standing by a large metal door set into the outside wall. The entire pool is covered by a metal building, keeping the weather out. It's also keeping us in, since this place is locked from the outside.

"Don't worry, my guy is supposed to be here." She sits, sliding her back down the side of the wall, feet sticking straight out in front of her. The gravel shifts under her boots, digging two shallow ruts.

I dig the toe of my shoe into the gravel, about to start asking her questions but thinking about how to start. No time like the present to grill her for answers since we're just sitting here doing nothing.

A triple knock sounds on the outside of the metal building.

knock, knock, knock

#thwarted

"I knew he'd be here." Kat grins then stands up again, leaning toward the metal wall. She repeats the knock that just sounded outside.

There is the sound of metal clanging, then a loud squeak, and the door eases open. Light streams into the darkness, and fresh air assails my nostrils, making me realize just how bad this place smells.

A boy stands in the doorway smirking at us; apparently finding us stinky and wet is pretty funny.

"Can it." She stops whatever sarcastic comment he was going to make. "Just be glad you weren't the one who had to go in the pipe with him. Just remember that this could have ended very differently."

He wipes the smile off his face and nods his head in agreement. "You got me, I'm glad to be on this end instead of that end." This time he does laugh, but Kat just ignores it.

I step forward, wanting to get the heck out of this building and the heck out of Dodge. I'd rather not give someone else a chance to take me hostage.

"I'm Jake." The guy at the door sticks his hand out, intercepting me.

I recognize him!

"You're the one who tased Dirk," I say, effusive. "Thank you so much! You totally saved my skin back there."

I reach out to shake his hand then remember that I've just climbed through a sewer. He doesn't seem fazed, but he does wipe his hand on his pants afterward. I guess he knew what he was in for.

He shrugs his shoulders. "It's no problem, I'm glad to help Thomas's brother. You need to get home, though, there's not a lot of time left." He glances up at the sky, and I wonder what he's looking for.

I'm about to ask more questions when Kat catches my attention.

"Come on," she says, grabbing my sleeve and pulling me along once again. She's jogging toward a high brick wall with a rusty metal ladder attached to it. Jake jogs behind us, and I feel bad for him, he needs to get upwind at the very least.

We congregate at the edge of the wall, and I realize with dismay that the ladder doesn't reach us. It's way too high for any of us to grab; maybe if we stood on each other's shoulders, but that seems pretty dangerous.

If we could reach it, though, it would be an ideal way to get out of the prison's compound.

While the ladder is about 10 feet off the ground, it's also equipped with an attached lever. The lever looks like it can be pushed to the side, allowing the ladder to slide down to the ground.

The question is how do we trigger that lever?

"How are we going to get up there, Kat? I don't know about you, but the last time I checked, I couldn't fly."

She levels me with a look that tells me I'm pushing my luck, so I step back, leaving the "doing" part of things to her and Jake. They wouldn't have brought me here without a plan. I swing my arm out wide toward the wall as though saying, "Well, go on then."

Jake's been silent up to this point, watching us banter back and forth.

In response to my hand motion he steps forward, reaches into the pocket of his overalls and pulls something out. His hand is wrapped around most of it, but, from what I can see, it almost looks like one of those retractable dog leashes. It would be for a very small dog because it's not more than three inches square. It's got a handle on one end and a hook sticking out from a retractable wire on the other end.

He extends his arm and begins rotating at his shoulder, like a freestyle swimmer. He swings his arm in wide circles two or three times, I'm assuming so he can gain speed. Then he releases the hook at the top of the arc and follows through as it flies through the air. The metal hook catches a rung of the ladder, wrapping around the bar and grabbing back on itself. The connection now appears to be secure.

Pulling his arm back and down in a quick motion, Jake tightens the loop on the ladder rung, holding it fast. Finally, he gives the handle a yank, the lever moves over under the pressure, and the entire ladder comes sliding down on its fixtures. The feet land on the soft earth without a sound.

Kat grins at me, waggling her eyebrows. "I told you he always comes through."

Jake smiles at both of us, blushing a bit and giving a mock bow. "I do like to make things easier when I can, ma'am." He drawls out his words in his best cowboy accent.

Kat heads to the ladder, stepping one foot on the bottom rung and bouncing on it, making sure it's steady. She climbs it like she seems to do everything else in this game, fast, with a single-minded purpose.

I would not be surprised to see someone standing at the top ready to hand her a gold medal and a bouquet of flowers.

#competitive

Jake gestures for me to go on ahead of him, so I do. But first I test the ladder with my hands, pulling hard on the rungs before trusting it with my weight.

I don't care at all that Kat made it up safely. Maybe she just loosened it enough so that it'll let go when I start climbing. This thing is not in good shape at all. Metal flakes prick my palms, and I have no doubt Jake will have flakes of it in his hair, courtesy of what I'm kicking off the rungs with my boots. I make it up safely, but my hands are covered in red rust by the time I join Kat on the ledge.

I look down at Jake as he comes up, thinking that maybe I can help him if something goes wrong. What I'd do I'm not exactly sure, but at least I'd know he was hurt and I could ... think of something.

He reaches the top without incident, though, and we all turn, facing away from the prison grounds.

We're standing on top of a very large perimeter wall. It might only be ten feet high but it's wide. Not "Great Wall of China" wide but probably 8 feet. Plenty of room for us to stand next to each other, plenty of room for guards to patrol, shooting any escapees on sight.

I glance around the wide open area, but there doesn't appear to be anyone out here with us at the moment, guards or escapees.

Looking out from the wall, I think of how many times I've escaped from this place while playing "Roblox". It's stressful when it's digital, but it's nothing compared to how it feels in real life.

Real life? Is that what this is? Is it really happening to me if someone else could see me on a computer screen in their game? What about Kat and Jake, are they really here with me? Or are they sitting at a desk, controlling their little pixelated people?

Enjoying some popcorn while watching me move around?

Once again, my questions are thwarted.

"You're going to have to jump," Kat says, turning to me and indicating the ground below, which now looks far, far, far away... "Jump down, and then follow the road until you reach the end of the game."

"The end of the game?" My voice sounds dull in my ears. They're about to leave me alone? I think I might pass out. What does it feel like when you're about to pass out? Breathe, Jed, breathe…

"How am I supposed to know where the end of the game is?" It comes out sharper than I intended, but whatever. They're treating me like this is just no big deal, but it is, it is a VERY big deal.

"You'll know, Jed," she says. "Just trust me on that. Head to town, that's where the road ends. Go to the jewelry store, the portal home is in there. You absolutely cannot miss it."

She takes me by the shoulders, something like my mom would do when she wants to make sure I'm really paying attention. "This is important, Jed. The most important thing."

I was right; it's exactly the type of thing my mom would do. "Once you get to the end of the game, you'll go back home, but you've got to get there before night time."

She looks over to Jake as though she's questioning how much she should say. He just crosses his arms over his chest and nods.

"Home before nightfall, Jed. Remember that. Because if you don't, you're going to be stuck here." She lets go of my shoulders, stepping back to look at me, trying to see if she's really getting her message through.

"'Roblox' swaps time with the real world, so if it's night here, it's day there," Jake says solemnly. "If you're not out of here by night time, you will not be back in your bed in the morning."

Wow, way to drop a bomb on a guy. I mean no pressure or anything.

"Okay," I say slowly. I look out over the endless fields and grass. Suddenly, town feels very far away. There's nothing to be done though. Yelling and crying and getting mad about it isn't going to get me anywhere, and it's sure not going to get me home.

"Well, I'll be on my way now." As nonchalantly as I can, I glance between the two of them. "Thanks for getting me this far."

I do wonder why they can't come with me. Somehow, with all of this information being shoved into my brain, I don't take the time to ask that question either.

I'm tired, weary to the bone. I'm sick of this place, done with being here, and afraid of what'll happen if I don't get back in time.

But mostly I'm worried about Thomas. What the heck has he gotten himself into, and why didn't he trust me enough to tell me about it?

"What about Thomas, where is he?" I look out over the fields again, as though he might be standing there.

If he's here, I know for sure I won't be leaving without him. I'm fully prepared to go back in there and do whatever has to be done.

"He's not here, Jed," Jake says. "He's hunting with your dad, didn't he tell you?"

"Oh man, I forgot about his trip." Kat aims another guilty glance my way.

That does sound vaguely familiar, now that he mentions it. I'm not much of a hunter, but Thomas loves going to the lease with my dad, especially during duck season, which started—this morning. Or it would have started this morning were I at home. Maybe that means it will start when I'm home.

I'm so confused.

Kat turns around again and confers quietly with Jake, who nods and reaches into the pocket of his orange jumpsuit. He pulls his hand out and gives me a slim, white plastic card.

I take it, or rather he lays it in my flat palm, and it sits there while I stare at it. It's almost weightless in my hand and looks like a white credit card. I see Dirk's (the jerk) name on it, written in black, block style letters.

Closing my fingers around the card, I put it in my pocket. My clothes are starting to dry from our swim, and the pocket is sort of stuck closed. I will NOT think about what it's stuck closed with.

"What is it?" I gesture, indicating the card they just gave me.

"It's a key card," Jake says, "the guards carry them, but if you're smart, you can steal one. You'll need it when you get to the end of the game. It's your way out."

Just like in the real game, I should have guessed.

"So I'll use this to get into the jewelry store, right?"

Kat and Jake smile at me, nodding in unison. "Got it in one," Kat says.

I shift from foot to foot, stalling, trying to think of a way to ask all my questions at once.

Trying to think of a way not to have to go out into that endless world all by myself...

Kat must sense my reluctance, but she's not going to let me off the hook. "Jed, you need to go now, there's no more time." She gives me a light shove in the direction of the ledge.

I turn and force my feet to move all the way to the edge until my toes are hanging slightly over.

I have to do this. I've got to get back home.

"Good luck, Jed," Jake says, a smile in his voice. "It was nice to finally meet you."

I nod, acknowledging his words without turning around.

"Thanks guys, thanks for all your help," I tell them.

Then I jump.

Chapter 8

Fields And Long Grass
As Far As The Eye Can See

I land in a heap on the ground at the base of the wall, smacking my head on the red brick when I lose my balance and fall backward.

Pain shoots up my leg, and I topple over, unable to hold my weight on my right foot. Man, this is the last thing I need right now. I know I've injured something, there's no doubt about it.

Looking up, I crane my neck to see if Jake and Kat are still on the ledge. I can't see anyone, the sun is blinding, but I call out to them anyway.

"Guys! Are you still there?" I think they should be; it hasn't been more than 30 seconds since I jumped, but I wait. All I'm met with is silence.

Trying again, I yell once more. "Guys... Kat! I hurt my ankle when I jumped; I think I'm going to need some help getting to town!"

I stop and listen, straining my ears, but no one responds. The only sounds I hear are birdsong and the whooshing of the grass as it sways in the wind.

They must have gone. I'm on my own.

I'm alone out here, there's nothing but grass and rocks for miles, and I'm alone.

Sitting there, I wait for the fear to hit me. I've got to get all the way into town, with a busted ankle, without being seen, before nightfall.

No big.

Instead of feeling scared, though, I feel determined! I am out of prison, that's the most important thing. I am NOT going back in, and if I have to hike for miles on a sprained ankle, so be it.

All gusto aside, my ankle really is messed up, and I do need to brace it somehow. Looking around again, I see absolutely nothing useful, so I decide to take the sock from my good foot and wrap it around my injured foot to keep it steady.

I remove my prison-issued orthopedic moonboots. Then I pull off my sock, thankful that it's not really that wet. I bind my sprained ankle tightly and put the boots back on. It's a really tight fit on one and a loose fit on the other, but it'll do. It helps a little when I open the laces of my shoe on the double-socked foot. I end up pulling the laces out of the top five holes and leaving the leather gaping wide around my calf.

Ah, blood flow. Being able to feel your toes is a good thing.

I can't bend my ankle much now, but I am able to stand and walk.

I'll take what I can get.

The foot doctoring complete, I get going. I'm slow and not entirely steady, but I figure I'll get to the road, which isn't too far away, and follow it to the end of the game. If I'm lucky, I might even be able to find a stick.

Looking around, I sort of doubt it since there isn't a tree in sight.

I remember from my time playing this as a video game (which I wish I were doing right now) that the road will take me to a city. I can then choose to parkour into various shops to wreak a little extra havoc or not.

I'm going to "or not" this time around, and I wonder how I ever enjoyed it in the first place. It's amazing how real life can cut the fun out of jumping 10 feet from one object to another.

I've been walking for a while, thanking my lucky stars for the road so that I can at least keep my bearings. Slowly, I start to notice the silence around me is no longer absolute. There's a humming, a sort of pushing buzz I've heard many times before in this game.

Someone is driving a car, and that someone is headed toward me on the road!

As quickly as I can with one lame leg, I duck into the high grass away from the shoulder. The car comes closer, and I hunker down. It's so loud, echoing off the small outbuilding a few yards in front of me, making me realize it's not just one car.

It's a whole convoy of cars!

I'm not dumb, I know there's only one reason why the guards would have mobilized an entire garage worth of cars and trucks, especially this late in the day. Most of the players are logging out at this point. They're eating dinner with their families and taking baths. They're finishing homework and getting ready for bed.

There's no reason for this sort of manpower.

These guys are here for me.

The convoy stops near where I am hiding, way too close for comfort, and I start to sweat, shifting a bit to ease the pressure on my sprained ankle.

The long grass pokes me in the face and neck. A piece with some grass seed still attached tickles my nose and I hold my breath to keep from sneezing.

Car doors open and close. The metal frames squeak as occupants get out, looking around, scanning the horizon. I hear footsteps on the asphalt and the scrape of boots on the ground. This is followed by the "shisk, shisk" sound of canvas uniforms brushing against long grass.

They're looking for me, and I know beyond a shadow of a doubt that I cannot let them find me.

Glancing around my hiding spot, I see a large rock just a few inches away. It's about the size of a golf ball, maybe a little more substantial. Perfect.

Pushing my hand through the base of the thick grass, I reach out slowly so as not to disturb anything. I pick up the rock, test its weight in my palm, and then throw it as hard as I can at the concrete outbuilding in front of me.

Never have I been so grateful for some random tool shed, or whatever it is.

The rock smacks the side of the building with a satisfying clatter, bounces off and drops to the ground, making even more noise as it rolls away from the slight incline the building was erected on.

I watch the guards; they follow the sound with their eyes then start running in that direction. They yell, "Go check it out; if he's there, we need to bring him in!"

Peeking up from my hiding place, I look at the convoy and rack my brain, trying to figure out how I'm going to get out of this mess. My day is saved when I spot what looks like a covered prisoner wagon in the convoy. Probably it's meant to haul me back once they find me.

Not today, guys.

#sorrynotsorry

It's a massive metal framed truck, about 2 feet off the ground. There are wooden benches on the interior of both sides of the truck bed, and a canvas tarp is strung tightly over metal poles bent at the top to shelter the bed occupants. I am pretty sure the truck is high enough for me to hide under.

I smile, knowing that I'll be there while the guards sent to capture me actually take me the rest of the way into town.

Creeping slowly toward that truck, I grin for the first time all day long. I just found my way out.

I'm under there.

Chapter 9

Jed Really Needs
To Get To Town

The crawl toward the convoy truck feels painfully slow. Scratch that, it actually is painfully slow. I make it, though, grateful for the stinky coveralls that protect my belly from the grass, rocks, and sticks that would otherwise tear me up. Even with my hindered ability, I make it there before the guards come back from their investigation of the outbuilding and the surrounding area.

My clothes are a mess; I'm covered in dirt and ... other stuff. I stink to high heaven, and my biggest fear right now is that the guards will stop and go, "What is that awful smell?" This would be followed by them investigating said funk and finding me and my hidey hole.

Looking under the truck, I see exactly what I was hoping to see.

The axles are set high enough off the ground that I can position myself directly above one of them, either hanging on to bolts in the frame or gripping the wheel well beneath me. I'll be over the wheel, away from the moving parts, and out of sight unless someone comes looking underneath.

I doubt they will, though, I mean who does truck maintenance in the middle of a manhunt?

It takes me a few minutes to get situated. Once I do, I'm surprised at how long I still have to wait before these guys come back. It must not be more than a few more minutes, but it feels like forever.

Eventually, though, I hear their footsteps and their grumblings.

Shucks guys, did you not find me? #suckstobeyou

"Keep going up the road," one of the guards says, "we'll catch up with him before he hits town." He sounds super confident.

"He's on foot; he's got to be going slow. One of those punk prisoners said he hurt himself when he jumped, that's not going to do him any favors."

Oh no. When I hear that last part, I feel shock and dread. They were caught, Kat and Jake were caught, or at least one of them was.

Please let them be okay.

Who knows how these guards got them to talk, I feel sick just thinking about it.

Don't think about it, I tell myself. *Get home, talk to Thomas, and figure out how to help them after that.*

It's all I can do, I'm no good to anyone injured, and especially not useful to anyone when I don't know what is going on.

If there's one thing I know right now it's that I don't know ANYTHING right now!

I adjust my grip on the bolts in the frame above the axle and hold on tight as the truck rumbles to a start and begins to work its way down the long prison road.

It's a long trip; this route must go for miles.

I don't know how I'd ever have made it on my own. A couple of times I smack my head on the metal frame when we hit a rut. It hurts, but it keeps me from dozing off and falling over. The steady drone of the engine coupled with the constant run of black asphalt in my vision is mesmerizing. I am so tired; the fatigue is starting to affect my brain. I feel muzzy and sluggish, and I can tell without looking at the light that it's definitely getting late.

When I do take the time to crane my neck and look, I can see the sun setting in the distance. It's a bright spot of radiant orange light perfectly placed between the bottom of the truck bed and the start of the land on the horizon. In about 30 minutes it'll be out of sight, and if I'm not at the end of the game, I'll be out of luck.

The grass and dirt go on for miles, a blur of brown and green speeding past. At first, the landscape is broken only by the occasional outbuilding, like the one I threw my rock at. As the time passes, more buildings come into view, their bases visible from where I'm lying.

The few buildings become many buildings, and many buildings become a town, complete with streets, signs, and fast driving cars. This is where the prisoners go to get cash. We rob the bank, rob the jewelry store, rob the train even, and use all that money to buy cool cars so we can steal things even faster.

Rebels, every one of us.

#thuglife

The truck finally rolls to a stop in the middle of town. The guards get out, making a ton of noise as they open and slam doors. The sound gives me plenty of cover to reposition myself without being noticed.

"Canvas the area." One guard barks out the order. "Find him, bring him back, failure is not an option. Trust me when I say that NONE of you want to go back and tell the boss we lost him."

Who is this guy that wants me so badly? What did I ever do to him? I'm 10, for Pete's sake! I am hardly in any position to do anything noteworthy at this point in my life, especially to some guy in a video game!

Holding my position for a few minutes longer, I take the time to calm down, slow my breathing and get a handle on my emotions. I can just imagine myself running across the street, half-crazed and scared out of my mind.

That would be a sure way to get caught.

When I'm ready to go, just to be sure I'm alone, I drop down from the undercarriage in stages. First I dangle my head down, looking to make sure I'm not missing any nearby guards. Then I let my feet down, allowing my throbbing ankle to get used to bearing some weight again.

It hurts so much worse now than it did even an hour ago. I look down at my foot, pulling my pant leg up so I can see what's going on. My ankle is so swollen that even the gaping leather cuff is starting to dig into my flesh.

I hope I can get these boots off when I'm back home.

Taking a deep breath, I lie on the ground beneath the truck and turn my head once more from side to side, checking for guards. When I don't see any, I roll out from underneath and get into a crouching position. It takes me a few seconds to get to my feet, and I have to force myself not to run. Instead, I walk normally, or as normal as I can.

I don't glance around, doing my best to look no more interesting than any other prisoner trying to rob the jewelry store. I see it just ahead of me on the right-hand side. There's a gigantic blue diamond set on the top of the awning, it glows brightly in the darkening sky, impossible to miss.

I pick up my pace as much as I can while touching my injured foot to the pavement as little as possible. My entire leg is throbbing. I'm so glad I've already come this far because I don't think I've got much left in me. The shadows are starting to spread, the sun no longer making headway among the tightly clustered buildings.

Finally, I'm there, in front of the store. There are two white "X" marks painted on the sidewalk in front of the doors. They let me know that, if I don't have a key card, I am not getting into this building through the front door.

Prisoners around the back, that's how it goes.

I send up a silent, "Thank you!" to Kat and Jake and then take the keycard from my pocket.

Placing the dark strip into the slot in the plastic reader, I pull down, running it quickly through.

There's a "snick" sound, a green light, and that's it.

No fanfare, no one comes running, no one is yelling for me to "STOP!"
I'm in.

Chapter 10

So Close To Home But Not There Yet

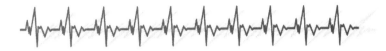

I was expecting something ... tougher when I finally got in here. Don't get me wrong, I'm glad there was nothing more, but it all feels a bit too easy, like I'm being baited.

After all, the further in I go the more limited my options for escape become. At least when I was outside, I could run away. In here I'm kind of in a fatal funnel, a rat in a maze.

One way in, one way out.

Still, this is where I have to be, so there's nothing to be done about the sick feeling. I'm going to proceed with caution, but I'm going to continue, period.

I look around, trying to figure out where I should be going.

It's not like there's a sign that says:

Portal
This
Way!

It actually looks just like any other jewelry store. My experience here is limited since I've never actually been in a jewelry store.

I imagine they all look sort of like the ones you pass in the mall. Long glass cases line the walls on either side, and there's a "kiosk" case in the middle. The cases are clear all the way around and on top so you can easily admire the sparkle and shine of the contents.

"Oooh, ahhhh."

That's my noise of admiration.

Behind the cases, lining shelves on the walls, there's more jewelry.

It's mostly things dangling from spinning racks. There are necklaces, long earrings, bracelets, pendants, even some rosary beads, and key chains.

Next to the spinning stands, there's a cash register. There's also a metallic looking apparatus that contains some type of liquid. Maybe it's used for cleaning things?

I see some small rings on long metal sticks, possibly for sizing people's fingers. There are even a few of those little magnifying glasses that jewelers use when they look at diamonds.

My footsteps are soft on the wall-to-wall carpeting as I make my way toward the back of the main room. It's freezing cold in here, and it makes me laugh when I think of people referring to diamonds as "ice".

It's icy, indeed!

The jewels and precious metals glint and shine under the bright, fluorescent lighting. There's a constant buzzing and flickering common to any room that has those types of light tubes hooked up.

I see a door at the back of the room. It's painted a glossy white in keeping with the "pristine" theme of the store and its contents. I place my hand on it, feeling its cold surface, then lean in and rest my ear on it, straining to listen.

Nothing, it's all quiet.

I guess if you got into the store with a keycard, the powers that be think you must belong here.

It feels like a substantial reason, but it also feels wrong, and it nags me. *It's just too easy,* my brain keeps repeating.

I put my hand on the shiny gold doorknob and twist.

Maybe it'll be locked. That actually might make me feel better.

I'd like knowing there's some sort of resistance that'll keep me from getting so quickly to my goal.

It doesn't resist. Instead, it turns comfortably in my hand, and the door swings open, just as smoothly and just as soundlessly.

The open door reveals a short hallway ending at another door, this one grey metal.

This door looks a little more ominous though. It's the same size as any other door, but it's got a red dome light in a wire cage mounted above the frame. Two bullhorn looking loudspeakers are also installed, one on either side of the light.

There's another card reader here in place of where a standard key lock would be, like in a hotel room.

Well, I think to myself, *at least I've got this part covered ... hopefully.*

Taking out my stolen keycard, I swipe it through the reader. It works! A green light appears above the reader, I hear a click, and I'm able to turn the handle.

The door opens, I step through … and chaos ensues.

Well, I did ask for some resistance.

The red light above the door starts flashing.

It's so bright I put my hand above my eyebrows like I'm shielding them from the sun.

Almost immediately, I take my hand down and use it to block my ear. The bullhorn speakers have made themselves known in a big way.

The noise is incredible! "WAAAAA! WAAAAA! WAAAAA!" It blares at me in stereo, and I know my luck has run out.

The guards will be here any moment, I'm sure of it.

The good news is that I can see the portal!

There's a large metal safe set into the far wall of the room, just like something you'd see in a bank. It's circular, a huge, round hunk of metal easily 10 feet high. Three-inch bars stick out of a center portion, waiting to be slid home and locked.

It's open, though, and that's all that matters! I do wonder why they wouldn't have locked it, especially if they knew I was coming.

All the better to lure you to our lair, little piggy, I think.

Yeah, my brain is right, it probably is a trap, but I'm here, and I'm going.

I hobble/walk toward the portal; it looks like it's made of jello or fog. Actually, it seems like a combination of the two, if such a thing were possible.

Fello? Jog?

Beyond that portal, though, that's what really gets my attention.

It's Thomas's room!

I can see his bed, his shelves, the pulsing Minecraft Redstone block, and even Ty!

Oh my gosh, my dog. I miss him so much right now.

I want nothing more than to be in my room, curled up in bed with him at my feet. I can already feel his furry, 100-pound body keeping me warm, toasty, and safe.

I don't know for sure if he can see me, but he's sitting in the room, staring at the portal. His ears are perked up, tail wagging hesitantly like he's not sure if me being in this place is a good thing or a bad thing.

Behind me, time has run out, the guards have arrived in force. I hear the main doors slam open, glass shattering with the force. Boots stampede down the hallway, so loud I can barely hear the guards yelling to one another.

"Stop him! Do not let him go through that door!"

It's now or never.

I lurch on my injured ankle, covering the last 10 feet to the portal, and propel myself forward, preparing to do a belly slide into Thomas's room.

Freedom! I'm there, I'm right there!

A firm hand on the back of my shirt jerks me backward, and I slip awkwardly to the floor. My ankle has given up, I can't walk any further, and I certainly can't run.

I look up at my captor and am not at all surprised to see that it's Dirk.

He sneers at me. "So close but yet so far, eh Jed?"

I glare at him, furious, madder than I have ever been!

"You'd think so, you little twerp, but you'd be wrong," I say, sending off waves of confidence I don't actually feel.

I am so close! I want to go home! I want to see my family again, my brother, and my dog.

My dog... He's right there! I look at the portal; it's so close I can touch it.

I've got one shot left, and I'm going to take it. Twisting around, I face Thomas's room and call my dog's name.

"Ty! Come here, boy, come here, Ty!"

My fingers reach toward the portal. Ty starts to bark, jumping toward me and back in those quick motions he uses when we're wrestling.

"Ty, Come! Come!"

He listens!

He jumps toward the portal, and, in that exact moment, I use my good foot to push my boot against the floor. The motion gets me close enough that my fingers pass through the jello fog.

It's all I need.

I wrap my hand around Ty's collar, feeling the reassurance of his fur against my knuckles, and give the command we use when we're playing tug of war.

"Ty, pull! Pull!"

He hears the command and reacts instantly, jerking me toward him as his spine bows with the effort of moving himself rapidly in a backward motion.

In this manner, he uses all of his strength to make his way across the floor of Thomas's room.

VICTORY!

Dirk's grip is no match for Ty's might! His grasp on my shirt falters; I slide across the floor of the safe and back into my own world.

My fingers reach out to the Redstone block, and I waste no time in grabbing it and flinging it hard against the wall, knocking loose the panel.

The batteries fall to the floor, the portal blinks out of existence.

I'm home.

Ty's a superhero, he has the mask to prove it.

Epilogue

What's That Paper Sticking Out?

I sit in my room, petting Ty.

He rests his sleek, black head against my knee. His brown eyes are closed in bliss, and his huge, pink tongue lolls, basking in my belly rubs and ear scratches.

He doesn't understand why he's gotten so many extra treats tonight, but he's sure glad to have them.

My mind wanders to the ordeal of the past few hours. As much as I don't want to think about it, I know I don't have a choice in the matter. Thomas is involved; therefore I'm involved.

We're brothers, it's what we do.

How do I get ahold of these people? Kat, Jake, not Dirk ... not him. I know she promised she'd get in touch with me, but what if she doesn't?

I put my head in my hands and glance down at the Redstone block, in pieces on the floor.

Something is peeking out from the corner of the block, like the edge of a piece of paper.

Maybe it was tucked inside the battery compartment or perhaps it came through the portal with me?

I have no idea.

I leave my chair and walk over to the block, crouching down, wary of what it can do.

It's silent now, no glow, nothing at all, just plastic and circuits. I remember what it did, though, or what I think it did, and I treat it with respect.

Or at least I treat it with a healthy dose of caution.

Reaching out a fingertip, I push the paper to the floor. I use the pressure of my finger to slide it out from under the block, toward my feet.

Bringing it up to eye level, I can see that it's a note, written with a quick, sloppy scrawl:

You did good, kid.
See you soon.

Kat

"See you soon? What does she mean by that?"

I'm pretty sure I'm about to find out.

Please leave a review,
they're so important.

The more reviews you leave,
the more books I write.

Ty

P.S. - Don't forget to download your free
short story at tythehunter.com

Next - The World Keepers - Book 2

Thanks to Buddy Poke
for letting me use their app
to make a lot of these characters.
You can make your own at
BuddyPoke.com

Made in the USA
Middletown, DE
19 December 2018